GRUMPY GRANDPA

For my father,
and for my son, Daniel
—H. H.

For Uncle Bob and Aunt Alice
—R. M.

Atheneum Books for Young Readers • An imprint of Simon & Schuster Children's Publishing Division • 1230 Avenue
of the Americas • New York, New York 10020 • Text copyright © 2009 by Heather Henson • Illustrations copyright
© 2009 by Ross MacDonald • All rights reserved, including the right of reproduction in whole or in part in any form.
Book design by Sonia Chaghatzbanian • The text for this book is set in Ed Gothic. • The illustrations for this book are
rendered in watercolor. • Manufactured in China • First Edition • 10 9 8 7 6 5 4 3 2 1 • Library of Congress Cataloging-
in-Publication Data • Henson, Heather. • Grumpy Grandpa / Heather Henson ; illustrated by Ross MacDonald. – 1st ed.
p. cm. • Summary: Jack's grandfather is always grumpy, and a bit scary, too, but during a visit to the country house
where "Grumpy Grandpa" lives with the brave Aunt Ellie and Uncle Wilbur, Jack learns that his grandfather was once
very different. • ISBN: 978-1-4169-0811-1 • [1. Grandfathers–Fiction. 2. Old age–Fiction. 3. Mood (Psychology)–Fiction.
4. Country life–Fiction.] I. MacDonald, Ross, 1957– ill. II. Title. • PZ7.H39863Gru 2009 • [E]–dc22 • 2008021543

GRUMPY GRANDPA

written by **heather henson**

illustrated by **ross macdonald**

atheneum books for young readers
new york london toronto sydney

I have one grandpa.

He is always grumpy.

I call him Grumpy Grandpa even though I'm not supposed to.

Mom gets mad, but it's true.

Grumpy Grandpa is **always** grumpy.

And he's scary, too.

Grumpy Grandpa has great big eyes.

And he has hair everywhere—everywhere except where it's supposed to be.

And he has teeth that never stay in one place.

Grumpy Grandpa yells at the newspaper.

He yells at the TV.

He even yells at his own dog sometimes. I've seen him do it.

Grumpy Grandpa lives way out in the middle of nowhere. I guess he has to, because he's so grumpy.

The only people for miles around are Aunt Ellie and Uncle Wilbur. They are very strong and very brave—like lion tamers.

When I was little, I thought Grumpy Grandpa lived in a zoo because of all the different animals he had.

I still think Grumpy Grandpa should live in a zoo.

We could put him in a cage next to the monkeys, and people would pay money to see him be grumpy.

There's not much to do at Grumpy Grandpa's house. And it's really quiet.

No honking horns. No fire engines. No car alarms. No ice-cream trucks.

"It's too quiet to sleep!" Dad always says.

Mom and Aunt Ellie and Uncle Wilbur always laugh.

Grumpy Grandpa never laughs. I don't think he knows how.

Most of the time I just try to stay out of
Grumpy Grandpa's way. I don't want to be yelled
at like the dog or the TV or the newspaper.

It's not as easy as you'd think.

He's quicker than he looks.

And another thing: You have to watch where you sit.
You never know where Grumpy Grandpa has left those teeth.

In the afternoons Grumpy Grandpa takes a nap.
Then everything has to be really, really quiet.
Everything except for Grumpy Grandpa.
He snores so loud, it's like a cave full of grizzly bears.
And he roars just like a mean old lion if something accidentally wakes him up.

Mom says that naps make you feel better.

But I don't think it's the same for Grumpy Grandpa.

I think naps make him feel worse.

After his nap Grumpy Grandpa always disappears.
The dog disappears with him. You'd think the dog would need a break, but he sticks to Grumpy Grandpa like glue.

Grumpy Grandpa drives pretty fast for somebody who doesn't see so well. He makes the chickens fly. (I didn't know chickens **could** fly.)

He makes the tractor fly, too. (I **know** tractors aren't supposed to fly.)

"Where does Grandpa go every day?" I ask Mom.

"I think he just needs some time alone," Mom says.

This doesn't make any sense to me. If he wants to be alone, why do we drive two whole days to get here and stay two whole weeks?

"Why do we have to come here anyway?" I grumble.

The next day, after his nap, Grumpy Grandpa doesn't just disappear like always. He takes me prisoner.

When we come to a pond I've never seen before,
Grumpy Grandpa heads for a tiny boat. Then he hands me a
fishing pole and tells me to **sit still**.

We **sit still** for a long, long, long time.

"Where are the fish?" I ask.

"Shhhh," Grumpy Grandpa says.

"Maybe they don't like worms."

"Shhhhhh."

"Maybe we should come back when it's not so hot."

"Shhhhhhhh!"

"Maybe we should have brought something to drink."

"Shhhhhhhhhh!"

"Maybe there aren't any fish in this pond."

"And maybe you're scaring the fish away with your yip-yapping," Grumpy Grandpa growls.

"And maybe I know why you have to be alone so much!" I growl back.

And then I stand up so I can run away. But I forget one thing: I'm on a boat.

And then I'm not on the boat anymore.

I'm in the water.

But I'm not alone.

I look at Grumpy Grandpa.

Grumpy Grandpa looks at me.

And then something strange happens.

Grumpy Grandpa starts barking. Just like the dog.

Bark. Bark. Bark.

Grumpy Grandpa is **laughing!** I didn't even think he knew how!

He sounds so funny, I start laughing too.

You'd think we'd get out of the pond right away, but we don't. We just sit.

"You know something?" Grumpy Grandpa says.

I shake my head.

"When I was little, I used to swim all the way across this pond."

I look at Grumpy Grandpa. I can't believe he was ever little. And I can't believe he could really swim all the way across this pond.

"And when I was little, I used to run across that field just to see how fast I could go," Grumpy Grandpa says.

I look at the big green field. I know Grumpy Grandpa's pretty quick sometimes, but I can't believe he could ever run.

Grumpy Grandpa reaches out and taps the boat. "And when I was little, I used to come fishing with my grandpa in this very boat."

I look at the boat. It must be really old. And then I look at Grumpy Grandpa. I can't believe he ever had a grandpa of his own. That guy must have been really, **really** old.

"Was your grandpa grumpy?" I ask.

"Sometimes," Grumpy Grandpa says.

"Was your grandpa scary?"

Now Grumpy Grandpa looks at me. "Maybe a little."

"But why?"

Grumpy Grandpa doesn't answer right away, and
when he does, it's not with a roar or a growl or even a bark.
It's more like the water in the pond. Soft and kind of . . . nice.
"Maybe sometimes he forgot what it was like to be little."

We climb back into the boat. I'm still not sure about fishing, but now I don't mind sitting so much. For some reason, Grumpy Grandpa doesn't seem so grumpy anymore. He doesn't seem so scary, either.

"When I was little, my grandpa and I used to sit here all day long just to see how many fish we could catch," Grandpa says.

"How many fish could you catch?"

"More than we could eat."

I look at my fishing pole. And then I look at the water.

"Are there really any fish in this pond?" I ask.

"You better believe it," Grandpa says.